A First Book of
Fairy Tales

Stories retold by
Mary Hoffman

Illustrated by
Julie Downing

A Dorling Kindersley Book

For Elliot Lassiter

DK

LONDON, NEW YORK, MUNICH,
MELBOURNE AND DELHI

US Editor Margaret Parrish
Senior Designer Sonia Whillock
Art Director Mark Richards
Jacket Designer Karen Shooter
DTP Designers Almudena Díaz,
Louise Paddick
Production Shivani Pandey

First American Paperback Edition, 2006
10 9
014-KN302-Aug/06

First American Edition, 2001

Published in the United States by DK Publishing, Inc.
375 Hudson Street, New York, New York 10014
Copyright © 2001, 2006
Dorling Kindersley Limited, London
Text copyright © 2001, 2006 Mary Hoffman

Library of Congress Cataloging-in-Publication Data
Hoffman, Mary, 1945-
    A first book of fairy tales/stories retold by Mary
Hoffman; illustrated by Julie Downing.--1st
American ed.
        p. cm.
    Contents: Cinderella--Selfish giant--Rupunzel--
Jack and the beanstalk--Sleeping Beauty--Little
mermaid--Frog prince--Beauty and the Beast--
Diamonds and toads--Twelve dancing
princesses--Fisherman and his wife--Princess and
the pea--Rumpelstiltskin--Snow Queen.
    ISBN-13: 978-0-75662-107-0
    ISBN-10: 0-75662-107-0
        1. Fairy tales. [1. Fairy tales. 2. Folklore.]
    I. Downing, Julie, ill. II. Title.
PZ8.H665 Fi 2001
398.2--dc21
(E)   2001028425

Reproduced by GRB Editrice of Italy
Printed in Singapore by Star Standard PTE
Discover more at
www.dk.com

Contents

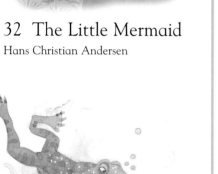

Introduction

What is a fairy tale? One thing we know for certain – there doesn't have to be a fairy in it. Of course, there often is a fairy – like the godmother in "Cinderella" and the wicked and good fairies who come to Sleeping Beauty's christening. But it is not compulsory.

What makes a story a fairy tale is a little bit of magic that stirs the imagination, and it doesn't matter where it comes from. It can be a pumpkin that is turned into a beautiful coach, a talking animal that can make a wish come true, or a spell that turns a handsome prince into a beast. Anything can happen in the world of fairy tales.

But a fairy tale is more than just a fantasy. There is often a strong moral lesson – kindness is rewarded, and greed and selfishness are punished.

A long time ago, long before people could read or write, storytelling already played an important part in their lives. Along with music making and dancing, stories were the main form of entertainment. And, although fairy tales are now treated as stories for children, originally they were listened to and known by everyone in the community.

All around the world, tales were handed down from generation to generation. Many fairy tales shared the same themes – good always triumphed over evil, and the central characters lived happily ever after.

When ordinary people started to read and write, the traditional stories might have been lost. But with the help of collectors who listened to them and wrote them down, fairy tales were preserved and continued to entertain children. Some of these fairy tales, such as "Cinderella" and "Sleeping Beauty," have remained as popular today as when they were first told hundreds of years ago.

I have chosen some of the best-loved and well-known fairy tales from the European tradition and added a sprinkling of the less familiar. I seem to have known them all my life, and I hope you will enjoy them as much as I do.

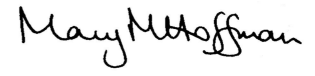

Cinderella

Once upon a time there was a nobleman who had a sweet wife and daughter. But his wife died, and his second one was horrid. She had two daughters whose bad tempers had given them ugly faces.

They were mean to their stepsister, Ella. She had to sweep the cinders from the grate, so they called her Cinderella.

One day, the king's son sent out invitations to a grand ball at the palace. The ugly sisters spent ages deciding what to wear. And Cinderella had to help them get dressed and brush their hair. There was no question of Cinderella going to the ball in her rags!

When the ugly sisters had left for the ball, Cinderella burst into tears. "How I wish I could go too!" she cried.

Suddenly, her fairy godmother appeared. "Don't cry child," she said. "Of course you can go to the ball! But first we'll need a few bits and pieces …

... bring me one pumpkin, six little mice, one large rat, and six lizards."

Well, Cinderella couldn't think how a pumpkin and some animals were going to get her to the ball, but she did as her godmother asked.

Her fairy godmother waved her wand and ... whoosh! The pumpkin disappeared, and in its place stood a beautiful coach. Then she waved her wand again. The six little mice turned into a team of handsome carriage horses. The rat was soon a rather fat coachman, and the lizards became six footmen.

So now Cinderella had
a lovely coach to take
her to the ball. But she
was still in her rags.
Her godmother smiled
and tapped her once with
her wand. Immediately,
Cinderella was dressed
in shimmering gold.

"Now, off you go," said her godmother.
"But, remember, at midnight everything will go back
to the way it was. So you must be home before then."
Cinderella promised, then stepped into her beautiful coach.
The six white horses set off toward
the king's palace.

Everyone at the ball
stopped dancing when the
mysterious stranger arrived.
Cinderella looked so beautiful
in her gold dress that everyone
thought she was a princess from
a foreign country. Even her
two stepsisters were fooled!

The prince was just as curious as everyone else. From the moment Cinderella came into the ballroom, he danced with no one else.

By the end of the evening he was madly in love with his beautiful "princess," and he didn't even know her name. And Cinderella was just as much in love with the prince.

But as they were dancing, Cinderella suddenly heard the chimes of the palace clock. "Oh no!" she cried. "It must be midnight."

Cinderella ran away from the prince, out of the ballroom, and down the palace steps, losing one of her glass slippers along the way. By the time she reached the bottom step, the clock had finished striking twelve and Cinderella was in rags again.

The prince ran after Cinderella, but all he found was the beautiful glass slipper from the steps. "Send out a proclamation!" he said. I will marry the person whose foot fits this slipper! We'll ask every woman in the kingdom to try on the slipper."

So the prince went to every house in the kingdom, and soon he came to the house where Cinderella lived with her stepsisters. Of course, the ugly sisters were very eager to try their luck. But no matter how hard they pushed their big feet into the slipper, it didn't fit.

So Cinderella came forward to try on the slipper. To the amazement of her stepsisters, it fit perfectly. The prince looked up at Cinderella's face and recognized the beautiful princess he had danced with at the ball. So he married Cinderella, and, unlike the stepsisters, they lived happily ever after.

The Selfish Giant

There was once a giant who wasn't nice at all. He went away to visit a friend and didn't come back for seven years. While he was away, children came to play in the giant's lovely yard. They were happy and forgot all about him.

Then the giant came back. "What are you doing?" he bellowed, and all the children ran away.

So the giant built a tall wall, and put up a notice, warning the children to keep out. At first the giant was pleased. Then he noticed that no birds came and sang in his yard anymore. And worse, it was always winter. The giant became sad.

Then one morning the song of a bird woke the giant. He looked out and saw that the children had come back. They had crept through a hole in the wall, and now the yard was full of flowers and birds.

The giant tore down the wall and promised never to be selfish again.

Rapunzel

Once upon a time there was a man and his wife who had the bad luck to live next door to a witch. They longed to have a child, and at last their wish was granted.

One day, the wife had a craving for some wild garlic, called rapunzel, growing in the witch's garden. Her husband picked some for her, and she ate it. The next day he went back for more. And on the third … the witch pounced on him!

"Why are you stealing my wild garlic?" she asked. The man explained that his wife had a craving for the plant. "Well, I shan't harm you, but you must give me the baby she is going to have," said the witch. The man, fearing for his life, agreed.

When the time came, the wife gave birth to a lovely baby girl. But the witch came to take the baby away. She was called Rapunzel, just like the wild garlic plant.

The witch brought up Rapunzel and, when she was twelve, locked her in a high tower that had no door or stairway.

Rapunzel had beautiful long hair, and when the witch wanted to visit her, she stood at the foot of the tower and sang,

"Rapunzel, Rapunzel, let down your hair, that I may climb without a stair."

And then she would climb up Rapunzel's hair.

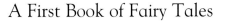

Years later, a prince was riding by the tower when he heard beautiful singing. He saw a lovely young woman at the window. Then he heard the witch's rusty voice calling and watched her climb up the cascade of hair.

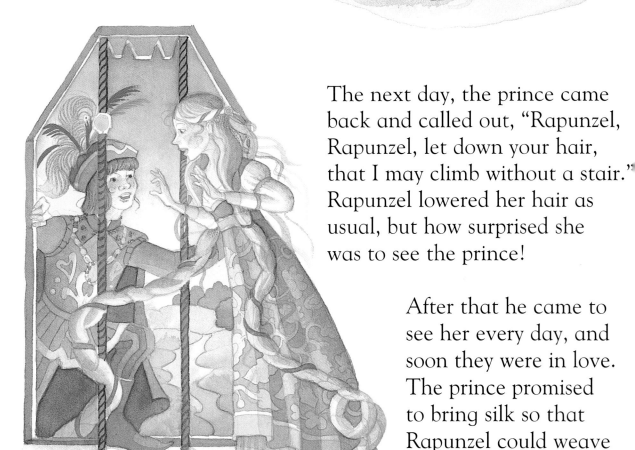

The next day, the prince came back and called out, "Rapunzel, Rapunzel, let down your hair, that I may climb without a stair." Rapunzel lowered her hair as usual, but how surprised she was to see the prince!

After that he came to see her every day, and soon they were in love. The prince promised to bring silk so that Rapunzel could weave a ladder and escape from the high tower.

But one day, silly Rapunzel said to the witch, "I wonder why you are so much heavier than the prince? It never hurts my hair so much when he climbs up to visit me."

Snip, snip! The witch put an end to Rapunzel's romance by cutting off her lovely long hair. How sorry Rapunzel was for her foolishness!

The witch spirited Rapunzel away and left her in a desert, where the poor girl wandered about, lost and alone. She had lots of time to feel sorry for letting the witch know she had a prince visiting her.

Meanwhile, the wicked witch had tied Rapunzel's hair to the window frame. When she heard the prince call, she let down the golden tresses as usual. Now it was the prince's turn for a surprise – and a very nasty one!

He tumbled down from the high tower, and the witch made him go blind. He crawled away, unable to see where he was going.

For years the prince wandered around the world, searching for his lost love, Rapunzel.

After a long time, he found himself in a desert. He was hot, tired, and thirsty. And then he heard a lovely voice singing such a sad song it made him weep.

"Rapunzel!" he cried. "Rapunzel, can it be you?" It was Rapunzel! She ran over to the prince and threw her arms around him.

When she saw that her prince was now blind, she cried. Her tears fell into his eyes, and suddenly he could see again.

Rapunzel and her prince were married, and they never saw the witch again. And Rapunzel's hair grew almost as long as before!

Jack and the Beanstalk

Many years ago there lived a woman and her son, called Jack. She gave him everything he asked for, until one day there was nothing left. All they had of any value was their old cow. So the woman sent Jack to sell her.

He hadn't gotten very far when he met a strange little man. "Where are you going with that cow?" he asked.
"To the market," said Jack.
"No need," said the man. "I'll give you these beans for her." Jack was such a foolish fellow that he agreed.

"One – two – three – four – five beans," the stranger counted out. And Jack ran home to tell his mother.

But his mother wasn't pleased at all. "You good-for-nothing boy!" she shouted and threw Jack's beans out of the window.

The next morning there was a marvelous beanstalk – as strong as an oak tree – growing right up to the sky. Without a thought, Jack climbed up it and found himself in another country.

He found a giant's castle and persuaded the giant's wife to feed him. But then he heard heavy footsteps and a loud voice saying,

"FEE FI FO FUM! I smell the blood of an Englishman!"

"Quick, hide in the oven,"
said the giant's wife.
The giant looked around,
but he didn't see Jack.
So he sat down to eat
his HUGE meal.
Then he called
for his pet hen.

From his hiding
place Jack could
see that the hen
laid an egg of solid
gold every time the
giant asked her to.

Soon the giant fell
asleep, and Jack rushed
out and grabbed the
hen. He escaped down
the beanstalk before the
giant woke up.

Jack's mother was very relieved to see him, and they lived well by selling the golden eggs.

But the beanstalk was still there, tempting Jack. Then one day, without telling his mother, Jack climbed the huge beanstalk again.

Everything happened as before.
The giant roared, "FEE FI FO FUM!
I smell the blood of an Englishman!"
This time Jack hid in a cupboard.
And again the giant couldn't find Jack.

After dinner, the giant got out his money bags and counted his coins. But soon he was asleep and snoring. Quickly, Jack grabbed a bag and slid back down the beanstalk.

Three years later, Jack climbed the beanstalk again.
This time he hid in a washtub when the giant roared,

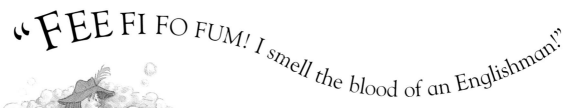

"FEE FI FO FUM! I smell the blood of an Englishman!"

The giant looked for
Jack, but did not find him.
Then the giant asked his
wife to bring the golden
harp. Soon he fell asleep.

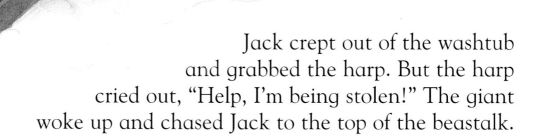

Jack crept out of the washtub
and grabbed the harp. But the harp
cried out, "Help, I'm being stolen!" The giant
woke up and chased Jack to the top of the beastalk.

But Jack was lighter than the giant and reached the bottom quickly. He flung down the harp and grabbed an ax to chop the beanstalk. It crashed down, and that was the end of the giant!

It was also the end of Jack's adventures. He lived happily with his mother, along with the hen that laid eggs of solid gold and the harp that sang beautiful songs.

Sleeping Beauty

There was once a king and queen who waited a long time to have a child. When at last the queen gave birth to a baby girl, they were so excited that they held a big party to celebrate her christening.

The king and queen invited all seven fairies in their kingdom, who came with very special presents for the baby. The king had solid gold plates, knives, and forks made for them.

But there was an eighth fairy who had been forgotten. She came stomping into the castle. Quickly, the servants laid a place for her at the table, but the plate, knife, and fork weren't made of gold! One of the younger fairies, sensing trouble, hid as soon as it was time to give the presents.

The first fairy gave the princess the gift of beauty, the second gave good temper, the third gave grace, the fourth gave a wonderful singing voice, and the fifth and sixth fairies bestowed gifts of dance and music.

Then the angry fairy said, "And when she is sixteen, she will prick her finger and die!" Imagine everyone's horror! But the young fairy in hiding came out and said, "She shall not die. She will fall asleep – and so shall all the court. After a hundred years, a prince will wake up our little princess with a kiss."

The next day, the king banned all needles from the kingdom. But when the princess was sixteen, she stumbled across a secret staircase in the castle. At the top was a woman spinning at a wheel. The princess had never seen a spinning wheel and wanted to touch it.

Immediately, the spindle pricked her finger and she fell down. Her parents found her and laid her on the best bed in the castle. Then they fell asleep too, along with the servants, cats, and dogs.

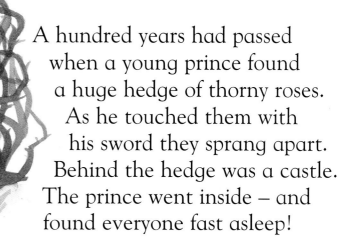

A hundred years had passed when a young prince found a huge hedge of thorny roses. As he touched them with his sword they sprang apart. Behind the hedge was a castle. The prince went inside – and found everyone fast asleep!

The prince roamed through the castle
until he found the room where the princess lay.
He bent down and kissed the sleeping beauty.
The princess smiled and sat up, astonished to find
the prince there. The prince and princess soon fell
in love. Meanwhile, everyone in the castle was stirring.
The wicked fairy's spell was broken at last! And as for
the prince and princess, they lived happily ever after.

The Little Mermaid

In the depths of the ocean, where the water is bluest, is the kingdom of the mer-people. It was here that the mer-king lived with his old mother and his daughters, the six mer-princesses, in the most beautiful palace you could imagine.

One by one, when they reached their fifteenth birthday,
the princesses were allowed to visit the world above the water.
The youngest princess couldn't wait for her turn to come.
At last, when it was her fifteenth birthday, her grandmother
said it was time for her to visit the human world.

The little mermaid rose above the foam and caught her breath in surprise. The world was so very much more wonderful than she had imagined.

All those on board were tossed into the water. The prince would surely have drowned if the little mermaid hadn't caught him in her arms. But she knew she couldn't take him back to her kingdom.

The first thing she saw was a huge ship. And on board there was a birthday party for a handsome prince. But while the little mermaid watched, a terrible storm blew up.

So she took him to the shore of an island, where a human princess found him. When the prince woke up, he naturally thought it was this princess who had rescued him. He knew nothing of the little mermaid.

But the little mermaid thought of nothing but the prince. She had fallen madly in love with him and longed to be his wife. "But he will never marry a princess with a tail," she lamented, "and how am I to get a pair of legs?" She set out to ask an enchantress who lived under the sea.

The enchantress gave her a potion, but the mermaid had to pay a terrible price. She would lose her beautiful voice and feel pain every time she walked. But worst of all, the mermaid would turn into foam if the prince did not love her.

The mermaid drank the potion and swam to the shore, where a dreadful pain split her tail and she found she had legs. The prince, walking along the shore, found her there and took her back to his palace.

The little mermaid became the prince's constant companion. She rode with him by day and danced for him every evening, even though the pain in her legs was like dancing on swords. But he did not love her.

The prince had never forgotten the other princess, the one he believed had rescued him from drowning. And now he decided to marry her.

The little mermaid watched the whole ceremony with a broken heart. She knew that she would turn into foam as soon as he kissed his bride.

Her sisters swam to her and gave her a knife to kill the prince. "It's the only way to save your own life," they said.

The little mermaid could not do it. She loved the prince too much. She kissed him goodbye and gave herself up to become foam.

But the spirits of the air took pity on her and whisked her up to live with them. They promised that if she did good deeds for three hundred years she would live forever.

The Frog Prince

There was a pretty little princess who lived in a castle near a dark forest. On hot days she liked nothing better than to play with her golden ball under the shade of the trees.

One day, she dropped the ball into a deep well. The princess wept bitterly at the loss of her ball. Suddenly, an ugly old frog appeared. "Whatever is the matter?" he asked. "I've lost my golden ball," she cried.

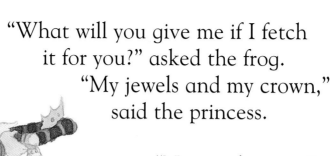

"What will you give me if I fetch
it for you?" asked the frog.
"My jewels and my crown,"
said the princess.

"No good to me,"
said the frog. "But if you
promise to love me and let
me eat from your plate and sleep
in your bed, then I will fetch it."

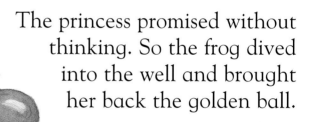

The princess promised without
thinking. So the frog dived
into the well and brought
her back the golden ball.

But as soon as she had it in her
hand, the princess ran toward home.
"Wait for me!" called the frog.

The princess forgot all about her promise. But the next day, when she was having dinner with her father, there was a knock at the door and in hopped the frog. The king made the princess tell him the whole story.

"Of course you must keep your promise," he said sternly. "Lift the frog onto the table." So the princess had to share her dinner with the frog, but it took her appetite away!

When it was time for bed, the king made his daughter carry the frog upstairs to her bedroom.

How the princess didn't want a cold, clammy frog in her bed!
But she knew that her father would be angry if she didn't
share her bed with the frog. So she let it hop onto her pillow.

"Now you must kiss me good night,"
said the frog. The princess
screwed up her face and closed
her eyes. Then she gave him
the smallest kiss. But when
she opened her eyes, the frog
had gone and in his place was a handsome
prince. "You've broken the spell," he said.

The prince was so grateful that he asked the
princess to marry him. And since she liked him much
better as a prince than as a frog, she said yes. He took
her to his palace, where they lived happily ever after.

Beauty and the Beast

There was once a rich merchant with three daughters. The two older girls were spoiled and wanted the finest things. But the youngest daughter was sweet natured and so lovely to look at that everyone called her Beauty.

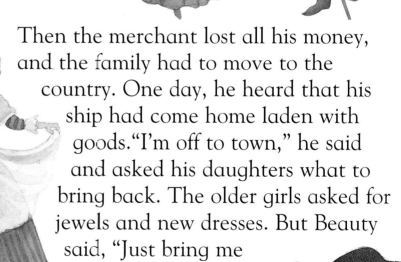

Then the merchant lost all his money, and the family had to move to the country. One day, he heard that his ship had come home laden with goods. "I'm off to town," he said and asked his daughters what to bring back. The older girls asked for jewels and new dresses. But Beauty said, "Just bring me one rose."

After selling his cargo, the merchant paid off his debts. But to his horror he found he had no money left at all.

The merchant rode home, feeling very sad. But along the way it started to snow heavily and he got lost in the forest. Then, the merchant saw a light. It came from a big house. He went in, but there was nobody about.

The merchant found a dining room with a blazing fire and a table laid for one. Since he was so hungry he ate …

a whole chicken, three delicious desserts, and drank a pitcherful of wine.

After dinner he explored the empty house and found a room with a comfortable bed already made up. He was so tired that he crawled into it and fell fast asleep.

The next morning the merchant found new clothes laid out for him. He got dressed and went for a walk in the garden. He saw a rosebush and remembered Beauty. "Just one rose," he thought, plucking it from the bush.

Then there was a mighty roar. "How dare you steal my flowers? I shall kill you for that," said the Beast. The merchant pleaded, and the Beast said he would spare the merchant's life if one of his daughters would take his place.

When the merchant got home
and told his daughters what had
happened, Beauty said right away,
"The rose was for me, father, so I shall
take your place. Let the Beast eat me."
Beauty's father wept. Even her sisters
managed to shed some crocodile tears!

Beauty trembled as she entered the Beast's house.
There stood the Beast, but instead of eating her
as Beauty had feared,
he welcomed her
into his home.

47

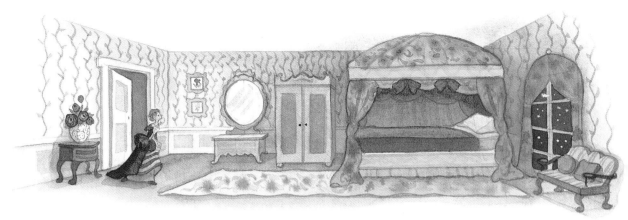

The Beast gave Beauty a wonderful bedroom,
with a magic mirror in which she could see
her old home whenever she wanted.

Gradually, Beauty
became fond of the
Beast, but she was
shocked when he
asked her to marry
him. "No," she
thought. "I cannot
love a Beast."
But he proposed
to her every day.

One day, Beauty looked into her magic
mirror and saw that her father was ill.
She begged the Beast to let her go home
for a visit. "You may go," he said. "But you
must promise to come back after one week."

Beauty found herself back at home by magic.
Her sisters were jealous of the beautiful clothes and jewels the
Beast had given her. "Let's keep her here longer than a week,"
they said. "Then the Beast will be angry and gobble her up."

But Beauty began to miss the Beast. One night, Beauty had a dream that the Beast was dying. So she wished herself back at his house. She went through the rooms looking for him, but they were all empty. Beauty ran out into the yard. And there, in the rose garden, lay the Beast.

He looked as if he were dying. "Don't die, Beast," she cried. "I love you. I will marry you!" And suddenly, the Beast was transformed into a handsome prince. He told Beauty that he had been put under a spell by a wicked fairy.

Beauty and the prince were married and lived happily ever after. And a good fairy turned the two older sisters into statues, which had to stand forever at their sister's gate!

Diamonds and Toads

There was once a widow with two daughters. The younger one was a good-natured girl who always had a smile on her face. The older girl was bad tempered and greedy like her mother, and they were always mean to the younger girl.

One day, they sent her to the well for water. There she met an old woman who asked her for a drink. "Of course," said the girl. Then the woman revealed herself to be a fairy and in return bestowed a secret gift upon the girl.

When the girl got back home, she was scolded for being late. And when she opened her mouth to explain, out fell flowers and diamonds and all kinds of precious jewels, for this was her gift.

"Quick, go to the well, too!" said the mother to her older daughter. The daughter went and met a young woman who asked her for some water. But the greedy girl refused. Then the fairy – for that was who she was – rewarded her with an unusual gift!

When the grumpy daughter returned home and opened her mouth to complain, to everyone's horror, out dropped toads and lizards and snakes!

The younger sister was thrown out of the house. But she was rescued by a prince, and when he saw how beautiful she was and what valuable things fell out of her mouth, he asked her to marry him. But no one wanted to be near the older sister. She lived alone for the rest of her life.

The Twelve Dancing Princesses

There was once a king who had twelve beautiful daughters. He was very fond of them and didn't want them to leave home. So every night he locked them in the bedroom they shared. But every morning he found their satin shoes worn out.

The king couldn't understand how this was happening, so he said that anyone who could discover where the princesses went dancing could marry one of them and become king. But no one could.

One day, a soldier came to town and read about the reward.

Solve the mystery of the worn shoes.

REWARD
Win the crown and a princess of your choice.

On his way to the palace, the soldier met an old woman. She told him not to drink the wine that the princesses would give him at bedtime. She also gave him a magic cloak to make him invisible, so that he could follow the princesses.

The soldier was made welcome at the palace, and given fine new clothes. But when he was given a cup of wine at night, he only pretended to drink it. Just as well, because there was a sleeping potion in it!

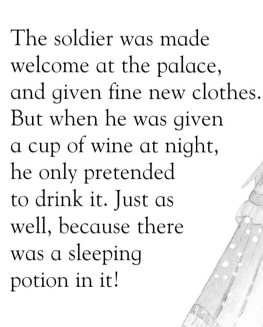

The soldier pretended to be fast asleep, but all the
time he was watching from the room next door.
He saw the oldest princess tap her bed
and a secret passageway appeared.
There was a staircase under
the bedroom floor!

The soldier watched as the princesses disappeared one by one. Then he leapt out of bed and put on the magic cloak, so that he could follow them without being seen.

In his haste, the soldier trod on the dress of the youngest princess, who was the last to descend the secret staircase. "Someone's tugging at my dress," she complained. "Nonsense," said her sisters. "There's nobody there."

Next, they passed another wood where all the trees were made of shimmering gold. The soldier snapped off another twig, startling the youngest princess again. "Surely you heard that noise?" she asked her sisters.

When they got out into the open air, the princesses walked
through a wood in which all the trees had silver leaves.
The invisible soldier snapped off a twig to take back
with him – the noise made the youngest princess jump.

Finally, they traveled through a wood where the trees were covered
with sparkling diamonds. The soldier broke off a diamond twig.
But when the youngest princess cried, "What was that loud snap?"
her sisters said, "It was a gun fired to welcome us."

On the other side of the diamond wood was a blue lake; twelve handsome princes stood ready, each waiting to row a princess across the lake to a castle. So the soldier quickly got into the boat carrying the youngest sister. When the sisters reached the beautiful castle, they danced the night away with their partners.

At the end of the night, the princes rowed the princesses back across the lake, and this time the soldier sat in the oldest sister's boat. The tired princesses went straight to bed, taking off their tattered shoes! The same thing happened the next two nights.

Then the soldier showed the king the silver, gold, and diamond twigs, and took him to see the secret staircase. The twelve sisters looked on in disbelief.

"Congratulations," said the delighted king. And just as the reward said, the soldier was allowed to choose a princess and inherit the kingdom.

The Fisherman and his Wife

There was once a poor fisherman, who lived with his wife in a hut by the sea. Every day he went to fish in the sea with his rod and line.

One day, he caught a huge flounder, who begged not to be killed. "I am an enchanted prince," it said. "I wouldn't taste nice at all. Put me back in the water."

When the fisherman came back home empty-handed, his wife scolded him, "Have you caught nothing today?" "Nothing but an enchanted prince," replied the fisherman. "And did you ask for no reward? Go back, you fool, and ask for a house!"

"Flounder, Flounder come to me," called the fisherman, and the magic fish came back.

"I'm sorry, but my wife wants a new house in return for saving you." "Go home," said the flounder. And the fisherman went home and found his wife in the sweetest little cottage.

But the wife wasn't satisfied. "Go back and ask for a castle," she demanded. So the fisherman went back to the sea and called the flounder again.

When he got home this time, he found a huge castle, with towers and a drawbridge. "This is more like it," said his wife.

But before long she
sent him back to sea
again. This time she
wanted to be the king,
and that night the
fisherman returned
to a king's palace.

Next, the wife wanted to be the emperor.
When the fisherman got back from that errand,
he could hardly find his wife in the vast imperial palace.

She was surrounded by guards and servants. "Surely you are happy now, wife?" pleaded the fisherman. She thought for a bit and then said, "No. I want to be God."

The fisherman went back to the flounder with a heavy heart. "She wants to be God," he whispered. "Go home," said the flounder. And when the fisherman returned home, he found his weeping wife – back in their poor old hut!

The Princess and the Pea

There was once a prince who was looking for a wife. Only a real princess would do, and he was very fussy about what she must be like. He went on long journeys to find the right one. But every princess that he found had something wrong with her.

One was bad tempered …

one was too tall, one wore silly clothes, and one had too many dogs!

Then one night, in the middle of a terrible storm, there was knock at the castle door. Outside stood a very wet and bedraggled girl, who said she was a princess. She certainly didn't look like one.

The queen had an idea. "We'll soon find out whether she's a real princess or not," she said. "I have a test that will prove it." She found a hard, dried pea. Then she invited the girl to stay the night.

After the girl had been given a hot bath and a dry nightgown, she was shown into a splendid bedroom. But the queen had put the dried pea on the bedstead, and ordered the servants to pile twenty soft mattresses on top of it.

In the morning, the poor girl
said she had had a dreadful night.
"I was so uncomfortable," she said.
"There was something hard in the bed,
and I tossed and turned all night.

"What a sensitive creature!" said the
prince. "Only a real princess could feel
a pea through so many mattresses."
So they married and lived happily
ever after. As for the pea, it was put
in a glass case in the palace museum,
and you can see it there to this day.

Rumpelstiltskin

Once upon a time, there was a miller who boasted to the king that his daughter could spin straw into gold. "Oh really?" said the king. "Then bring her to me. Such a skill will be very useful in my palace."

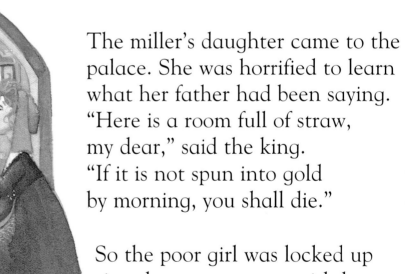

The miller's daughter came to the palace. She was horrified to learn what her father had been saying. "Here is a room full of straw, my dear," said the king. "If it is not spun into gold by morning, you shall die."

So the poor girl was locked up in a large storeroom with lots of straw and a spinning wheel. She had no idea what to do, so she burst into tears.

Suddenly, a funny little man appeared and asked what was the matter. When she told him, he said, "What will you give me if I do it for you?" "My necklace," said the girl, and the little man agreed.

The little man set to work and soon the room was full of reels
of gold. The miller's daughter looked on in amazement.
In the morning the little man disappeared.

When the king came in,
he was delighted with
the girl. But he was greedy,
too, so he gave her an even
larger room full of straw
to turn to gold.

The girl was even more desperate.
Then, as if by magic, the little
man appeared again.
"What will you give
me this time?" he asked.
The girl gave him her ring.

But on the third night, when she was locked in a huge barn, she had nothing left to give the little man. "I'll take your firstborn child if you marry the king," he said.

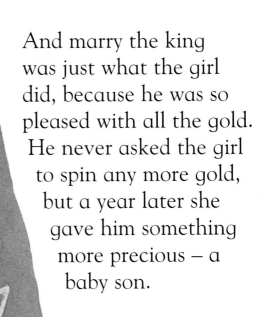

And marry the king was just what the girl did, because he was so pleased with all the gold. He never asked the girl to spin any more gold, but a year later she gave him something more precious – a baby son.

The queen had forgotten all about her promise to the little man. Then one day he appeared and demanded the baby. She was so upset that he took pity on her and said, "If you can guess my name within the next three days, you may keep the child."

For two frantic days the queen guessed, "Casper, Melchior, Big Ears, Balthasar, Bottlenose …?" But nothing was right. So she sent her servants out far and wide to search for unusual names.

The next day, a servant came back and said he had seen a funny little man capering round a fire in the forest, singing,

"I'll win the baby and the game. Rumpelstiltskin is my name!"

So when the little man came back, the queen said, "Is your name Wayne? Is it Darren? Is it perhaps ... Rumpelstiltskin?"

The little man jumped up and down with rage. "Who told you? Who told you?" he roared, stamping his foot on the ground so hard that it went straight through! He disappeared and was never seen again.

The Snow Queen

Once, there was a boy called Kay and a girl called Gerda, who were best friends. They were as close as brother and sister, and they lived next door to each other. Roses grew in the window boxes of their two houses and entwined together. In the summer, the children could sit on their balconies and talk to each other. In the winter, they played in each other's houses.

One winter, when Kay was visiting Gerda and her grandmother, the children were reading their favorite book by the fire. Suddenly, Kay called out in pain. "My heart" he cried, "and my eye!" From that moment on he didn't want to play with Gerda any more.

Two splinters of glass from an evil magician's mirror had pierced Kay's heart and eye. Now his heart was as cold as ice.

One day, when Kay was playing on the ice, he tied his sled to that of a mysterious stranger.

It turned out to be the Snow Queen, and she wouldn't let Kay go. She carried him away to her palace.

Gerda couldn't understand what had happened to Kay and searched for him everywhere. In the end she left their village, determined to find him.

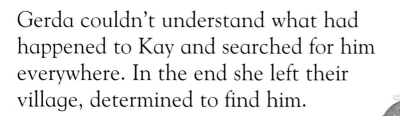

After weeks of searching, she met a talking reindeer, who promised to take her to the Palace of Ice, where the Snow Queen was keeping Kay as prisoner.

Gerda had never been so cold in her life. The palace was made of ice. She ran through halls of icicles and corridors of packed snow, until she came to a vast room with a frozen lake in the middle.

And on the lake sat her old playmate. "Kay!" cried Gerda, but he did not know her. Gerda ran across the lake, slipping and sliding. "It's me, Gerda," she said. But still he did not recognize her. Gerda could not bear it.

She started to cry and her hot tears fell on Kay's chest, melting the splinter of magic glass inside his heart. Then Kay cried too, and the splinter in his eye was washed away. Now they were friends again.

Kay and Gerda returned home. Gerda's grandmother was waiting for them, and the roses were in full bloom. When they looked in the mirror Kay and Gerda saw that they were now grown up. But they still felt like children at heart.

About the Storytellers

We know the names of some of the people who made up the stories in this book. But others have been collected from people who heard them from their grandparents and passed them on to their own grandchildren.

HANS CHRISTIAN ANDERSEN (1805–1875) wrote "The Princess and the Pea," "The Little Mermaid," and "The Snow Queen," among many others. He made them up, but based some of the ideas on stories he heard as a child in Denmark.

MADAME DE BEAUMONT (1711–1780) was a Frenchwoman who became a governess in England. The English version of her "Beauty and the Beast" came out in 1761 and became the best-known version of this tale, which has its origins as far back as AD 100.

THE BROTHERS GRIMM (Jacob 1785–1863 and Wilhelm 1786–1859) collected their fairy tales from ordinary country people. They published three volumes of tales (in 1812, 1815, and 1822) using the language of the German village people.

CHARLES PERRAULT (1628–1703) wrote his own versions of "Cinderella," "Sleeping Beauty," and "Diamonds and Toads" in 1697. They were translated into English in 1729 and became very popular.

OSCAR WILDE (1854–1900) wrote many wonderful plays and stories for grown-ups. "The Selfish Giant" is one of the nine fairy tales he made up and published between 1888 and 1891.

TRADITIONAL ENGLISH TALES
"Jack and the Beanstalk" is one of many traditional English tales that form the basis of the Christmas plays. It first appeared in print in 1807, but was known for at least seventy years before that. No one knows who made it up.